HŌPE
A Blueprint for Healing

By

Matt Nightingale

Page intentionally left blank.

Dedication

To both of my children, whom I have always loved,

and will continue to adore forever, totally
unconditionally

Table of Contents

INTRODUCTION

A Life Shaped by Trauma

The first sound was an alarm piercing through the terminal at Heathrow Airport. I had been running, desperate to find my father. The locked emergency exit door I rattled furiously, refused to give way. And the next thing I knew, security swarmed, hands gripped my arms, and I was pressed down in front of strangers whose eyes registered shock, judgment, and even pity. My humiliation burned as loudly as the sirens. To anyone watching, it may have looked like reckless behaviour, but for me, it was the beginning of a nightmare I couldn't yet name.

The police then became involved because I had inadvertently crossed from "Landside" (before you check in and go through security) to "Airside" (after all of that), which is illegal and something a terrorist might do, for example.

They therefore took me to a nearby station. I was dazed and confused, not really aware of what was happening. Before long, they put me in a cell for the night. However, 3 of them came in to do me serious damage. They each punched me many times, and threw me around the cell. I ended up on the floor, my shirt torn into 4 pieces. They knew where to hit me so that they wouldn't leave marks.

Because of this, my parents came back to the UK. They took me home, and a doctor was called to help. He gave me some very strong sedatives so that I would sleep for about twelve hours, as I was still full of energy. Unfortunately, the sedatives did not work because my system was firing on all cylinders. I only slept for four hours and woke up in the middle of the night. Again, without really thinking, I took my car to London to see my girlfriend. She had no idea I was coming.

The journey there was extremely dangerous. I should not have been driving in my condition. On the motorway, I drove at 70 mph and believed that I had a sixth gear, which I did not. I kept trying to put it into that gear, but there was no sixth gear. I was actually trying to put it into reverse. That is how confused I was.

What came next was even more surreal and incredibly dangerous. I was trying to reach my girlfriend, who was living just off Tottenham Court Road — one of the largest one-way streets in London, busy with traffic even in the middle of the night. When I reached the junction, there was an arrow on the road clearly showing that traffic could only turn left. But I was hallucinating, and I could have sworn it was pointing right. When the lights turned green, I turned right and drove in the wrong direction, dodging cars coming straight at me.

Once again, I was arrested, but this time not beaten. My parents arrived and, after some discussion, were allowed to take me home. That night was not a mistake of poor judgment or youthful carelessness. It was the physical manifestation of something far more terrifying. My first bipolar episode was at the age of 20. What began as disorientation quickly turned into a storm that would completely redefine every part of my life.

In that moment, I didn't have the language for what was happening. All I knew was fear and shame. And a sense that something inside me had broken loose.

This was the first of two occasions when I was "sectioned"— formally and legally detained in a hospital for assessment or treatment, even without consent. This is a legal process that can happen if you are deemed a risk to yourself or others due to a mental disorder. It was an incredibly traumatic experience, surrounded by other people with similar struggles.

Fortunately, I have only had 3 episodes in 30 years. The second did not require sectioning, as it was not as severe. However, the days of depression number in the thousands. A result of being 'ghosted' by my first daughter for the last 10 years, and my youngest for 3, as well as many times before that. The reasons are not always clear. It is not a rational choice or decision.

A first episode is always a terrifying surprise, whether it be high anxiety, deep depression, bipolar, PTSD, or many other conditions which are usually triggered by trauma. You are totally disorientated and not yourself at all.

95% of my life has been fairly normal, often extremely happy. The point is that mental health can destroy the other 5% (in my case), with disastrous consequences, the biggest being having to start all over again every time (finding a new job, for example).

This book is my attempt to piece together that story, not to glorify the pain but to make meaning of it. *Hope: A Blueprint for Healing* is an autobiography born of both struggle and survival. It is written with four purposes in mind. First, to pull back the veil of stigma that still shrouds mental health, especially bipolar disorder. Second, to raise support and funds for therapy, for young people who suffer in silence, believing they are alone. Third, to highlight the hideousness of what is now called Parental Alienation. And fourth, probably most importantly, to call forward the healers, therapists, psychiatrists, counsellors, and compassionate listeners, whose work can make the difference between despair and hope.

This is not simply my story. It is an invitation to listen differently, to speak openly, and to believe that even in the darkest of times, a thread of hope can still be found.

A Note About
bipolar disorder/ "Manic Depression"

Most readers will probably not be that familiar with this condition, even though 1.3 million people in the UK suffer from it (that's roughly 2%), and it is considered one of the most common serious long-term mental health conditions in the UK.

On top of that, it is not exactly the same for every person who suffers from it.

I simply want to explain that, in my case, I have only had 3 manic episodes in 30 years, always followed by a massive depression which lasts for much longer (months, sometimes years).

However, on top of that, I have suffered from far more depressive episodes (without the mania beforehand). I have suffered literally thousands of times, as you will read later on in the book.

Part 1
From Ecstasy to Agony

CHAPTER 1

A Happy Little French Boy

My childhood in France felt as though it had been painted with pastels. Each memory carries the sense of safety, routine, and joy. The kind of joy one rarely questions because it feels like the natural order of things.

Those early years were defined almost entirely by joy. The ease of childhood, filled with belonging and laughter, made any moments of fear or dislocation feel sudden and jarring when they arrived. Even the smallest surprises or changes felt sharper against that backdrop of safety.

The days followed a rhythm as steady as a heartbeat. Familiar streets where the smell of warm baguettes drifted from bakeries and mingled with the sharper scent of roasting coffee. Everyone knew everyone. Shopkeepers nodded when they saw me. Neighbours waved from windowsills. And there was a sense of belonging woven into even the smallest gestures.

Some of my clearest memories are not of celebrations or special occasions but of the small, everyday rituals that defined my early life. I remember getting on and off the bus to school with my sister, our hands clutching the cold metal rail as we climbed aboard. For me, that journey was a kind of reassurance. Life was orderly and predictable. I had friends to greet me at the stop, games to play at recess, and an uncomplicated sense that the world made room for me exactly as I was. Childhood was not something I thought about. It simply was, and it was very good.

Home was the true anchor. My parents filled it with warmth, their voices rising and falling in the steady music of English conversation. The house was modest, but it was alive with colour and noise. We ate simple yet rich meals around the table together. Afternoons were marked by games and evenings came with slower rhythms. The dimming light that pooled across the floor as we readied ourselves for bed. Sleep came easily in that cocoon of familiarity.

12 years in France gave me the gift of identity before I even knew what identity was. Belonging was not something I had to strive for. It was the air I breathed. I was seen and I was understood. I speak both languages fluently, and learnt them at the same time because my parents spoke English at home and we went to a normal French school, so we were always completely bilingual.

It was, in so many ways, the perfect beginning. And perhaps that is why the rupture to come felt so sharp. For in one moment, I had everything that made me feel whole. And in the next, I was stripped of it. The announcement came suddenly. My sister and I were being sent to boarding school in the UK (a foreign country to us, as we had spent almost no time there in 12 years). My parents spoke of opportunity, of the chance for something more in the United Kingdom. But to me, the words felt sharp-edged. Moving was not an adventure. It was a dislocation.

I said goodbye to my friends with words that caught in my throat, promising we would see each other soon. Even at that young age, I sensed those promises were hollow, that distance would erase them quickly.

There is a particular loneliness in being a child displaced from his home. My sense of self began to wear away. In France, I had been part of the group. Here, I was the outsider. Each day, the threads that had once held me together seemed to fray, and the world that had once felt familiar began to slip away. The transition was abrupt, not gentle or gradual. The child who had once felt secure, loved, and competent was now adrift. And though I did not yet have the words for it, I was beginning to unravel.

In France, I had been confident and capable. In England, I felt uncertain and small. The foreign boy fumbling to fit in. It was as though a mirror had been shattered, and I no longer recognised the child staring back. However, 18 months later, I earned an Academic Scholarship to my next school, which paid for 50% of the exorbitant fees. I worked very hard for that, and was proud to have achieved it.

Looking back, I see that all of this was the beginning of my unraveling. It did not happen all at once. It was slow, steady, and relentless. Each day added another thread pulled loose, another part of myself lost to the strangeness of my new world.

The loss of friends, of familiarity, of the comforting rituals of home, compounded until I felt hollow. The games that once brought me laughter were gone. The bus rides that once reassured me now belonged to a past that seemed unreachable. I learnt quickly that the world could change without asking me, that belonging was not a guarantee, that identity could be dismantled by forces beyond my control.

I was too young to articulate it, too inexperienced to name it, but I felt it in my bones. The world was no longer safe. Childhood had ended, not with a gentle transition, but with a rupture.

That is how it began, the unraveling of the self I had once known. And though I did not yet know the storms that lay ahead, this was the first fracture, the first, the first sign that my life would be defined not only by moments of belonging, but by profound moments of loss.

CHAPTER 2

The Boarding School Prison

The memory of that first day remains foggy. It was not the kind of day that can be recalled through neat details. What I remember most is the feeling: a dense, suffocating confusion that wrapped itself around me and refused to lift. It was the beginning of a quiet kind of loss that settled deep and never fully left.

There was no single moment of arrival, no welcome, no anchor. One day I was home, the next, I wasn't. The rhythms that had defined my world, the smell of my mother's cooking, the sound of my sister laughing, were gone. In their place stood a new order. Cold dormitories, echoing corridors, and unfamiliar faces.

I remember standing in the first hall, the walls painted in that institutional beige that seems designed to erase warmth. Boys spoke too loudly, as if noise could fill the emptiness. My sister had been sent to another school altogether a long way away, and it was as if she had vanished from the world. We had always been together, two halves of the same childhood. Now there was only absence. I caught myself scanning the room for her, even when I knew she wasn't there.

Everything about boarding school felt foreign. I tried to learn quickly, but the rules were unspoken and unforgiving. My first mistake came at breakfast. I lifted my bowl of cornflakes and drank the milk straight from it, as I always had in France. The table fell silent. A few surprised faces, a few stifled laughs. It wasn't cruel, just enough to mark me out as different. I felt myself shrink.

The days were long, but the weekends were worse. It was a weekly boarding school, and almost everyone went home on Friday afternoons. The place emptied like a drained vessel, corridors silent. Only two of us remained, another boy whose parents lived abroad, and me. The silence of those weekends had a weight to it.

Over time, I learnt to move through the days with a kind of numb efficiency. I copied the others. Their jokes, their posture, even the way they carried their books. I wanted to blend in, to be unremarkable. Sport helped. I threw myself into rugby and cricket, sports I barely understood. For those brief hours of movement, I felt something like belonging. The noise, the running, the sting of cold air pulled me into the present. When the games ended, the silence returned, but now it was more manageable.

Nights were the hardest. The dormitory was vast, lined with metal-framed beds. I would lie there in the dark, trying not to cry, but the tears came anyway. Quiet and hidden in the pillow. I didn't want to be noticed, yet I knew the others could hear. No one said a word. In that silence, I felt both exposed and invisible.

The ache of missing home grew sharper each week. I began to dream of escape, of hearing my mother's voice. Desperation made me bold. I started breaking into the deputy Headmaster's office to use the telephone. Each time my hands shook as I picked the lock. When I heard the dial tone, my heart lifted. When she answered, I begged her to let me come home. I don't remember her words, only the distance in them. Perhaps she thought it was for my own good. But the silence that followed told me otherwise.

I did it again and again, half a dozen times at least, until even hope felt foolish. Each failed call left me smaller, hollower. The fear of being caught no longer mattered. What I wanted was connection. The deputy Headmaster's office became, for a while, a portal to another world. When that world stopped answering, I stopped trying.

There was no dramatic collapse, just a quiet surrender. One night I realised that no one was coming. The crying stopped soon after. I learnt to live with the emptiness, to conserve energy, to endure. From the outside I looked like any other boy. Obedient, polite, and ordinary. Inside, I had already begun to build the walls that would one day keep me safe, and also keep others out.

Years later, when I looked back, I saw that the experience had given me more than pain. It taught me endurance, yes, but also observation. I learnt how to read people, how to find warmth in small places, how to carry on. Those lessons, born of loneliness, would become tools for survival in a life that was still to unfold.

The school itself feels distant now, more memory than place, the echoes faded. But sometimes in dreams I am back there. A small boy at a window, watching others leave for the weekend. The ache in my chest is still familiar, but softer now. What remains is not only the memory of isolation, but the knowledge that even in absence, something in me refused to give up.

CHAPTER 3

Freedom at University

After the turmoil of boarding school, university felt like sunlight after a long winter. At 18, I managed to get a place at the London School of Economics, and the sense of freedom that came with it was overwhelming. For the first time in years, I could breathe without permission. I was still away from home, but London was a different kind of world. It was alive, unpredictable, and full of movement. There were no borders here, only possibilities.

That first year was pure lightness. Everything felt easy. I met some wonderful people, many of whom remain my closest friends even now, decades later. They became my chosen family, the kind that understands you without explanation. We didn't take our studies too seriously. Lectures were more about conversations between ourselves than whatever was being said at the front. We didn't party hard, but we laughed often. The happiness came from being young, free, and surrounded by people who felt the same way.

The second year began with that same sense of ease. I moved into an apartment with three friends in a nice part of town. We thought of it as our own small kingdom, a sign that we were finally living on our own terms. The first term passed smoothly. We worked a little, enjoyed life a lot, and carried on with the quiet certainty that everything was exactly as it should be.

But in the second term, something changed. That was when I experienced my first episode of manic depression. It arrived suddenly, without warning, and turned everything upside down. One moment I was my usual self, steady and composed, and the next, I was swept up in a rush of energy and confusion that felt completely beyond my control. What mattered was that it came out of nowhere and left me unrecognisable, even to myself.

I still don't know exactly why it happened. I suspect the earlier traumatic transition from my French day school to the English boarding schools had a lot to do with it. The emotional dislocation of those years must have left cracks beneath the surface, and now they were beginning to show.

The experience was terrifying. I didn't understand what was happening to me, only that it felt entirely alien. Suddenly, that part of me disappeared. Breaking through the emergency exit at Heathrow, being physically assaulted by the police, and then driving the wrong way down one of London's largest one-way streets,

Tottenham Court Road, felt like living someone else's life. To be sectioned afterward, locked away, made it feel as if everything I thought I knew about myself had come undone.

Because I had been sectioned, I vanished from the university overnight. One day I was there, the next I was gone. My friends had no idea what had happened. I was taken to hospital still caught in the manic phase, detached from reality, unaware of what was real and what wasn't. When the mania passed, the depression arrived, which was deep, heavy, and unrelenting.

Eventually, after months of recovery, I returned to university. By then, my friends were a year ahead of me, but they welcomed me back as though no time had passed. The happiness of being back among them was immense. Life began to feel normal again. The laughter returned, the routine, the lightness that comes with being young and alive.

That return marked the beginning of a quiet renewal. I was back to myself, whole again, ready to move forward. The darkness had left its mark, but it hadn't taken away my sense of hope. If anything, it had deepened it. I had seen how quickly life could turn, and that made every ordinary moment, every conversation, every laugh, every lazy afternoon, feel like a small miracle.

CHAPTER 4

Happiness of Marriage and Children

Love began quietly, in a way that almost slipped past me. I met Vivian on holiday in France through mutual friends, and from the first moment there was a pull I couldn't ignore. It wasn't only physical; it was something deeper, something that felt both new and familiar at once. We didn't act on it then, but the memory lingered. A year later, at a party, our paths crossed again. The same connection was still there, though again nothing was said. Then one night, when I saw her across a crowded pub and waved, she waved back, and something lifted in me. My heart soared. We didn't speak that evening either, but I asked a friend for her number afterwards. I couldn't let it pass a third time.

Our first date was in London. I cooked dinner for her, nervous and excited. We spent hours talking, sharing food, laughter, and that sense of discovery that comes when two people are falling into something real. I distinctly remember going for a short walk down to the river Thames and admiring the beautiful lights on Chelsea Bridge.

From there, things moved quickly. We were young, caught up in the intensity of it all. I was 24 when we met properly, 25 when I proposed, and 26 when we got married. Between those moments, life was a blur of joy and motion.

There were small memories that still feel vivid now. Like for Vivian's birthday, I once gave her an envelope that said she had 'earned' one hundred Ben points, like frequent flyer miles, and had now qualified for a trip to France. She laughed when she read it, and that laughter felt like the sound of sunlight. We went to France together soon after, driving along the coast with the roof down, staying in small places on a low budget, deliriously happy.

When I proposed, it was at my mother's house. She said yes with tears in her eyes, and it felt as though the world had turned itself towards us. I knew she understood my struggles with mental health, and her acceptance of that part of me was deeply moving. We believed love could make us whole, and for a long time, it did.

Our wedding took place in Sussex. It was beautiful, full of colour. Her students sang in the choir, their young voices filling the church with warmth. When she walked down the aisle in her white dress, everything else disappeared. My mother couldn't be there because she had recently discovered she had throat cancer, but we raised a glass to her later at the reception. When it was time to speak, I felt my throat tighten because I was nervous. A tear slid down my cheek, not from fear, but from joy.

Our honeymoon was a dream. I was working for British Airways then, and they upgraded us to Business Class because it was our honeymoon. We flew to the Caribbean, stayed in beautiful places, walked along the beach, splashed in the waves, and kissed like the world belonged only to us. For 2 weeks, and for almost 8 years after that, life felt radiant. We were inseparable, bound by love and laughter.

When we returned home, life settled into its own rhythm. We moved in together, built a home filled with small routines and shared moments. She wanted to be a stay-at- home mother, which was becoming rare even then, but I agreed without hesitation. I adored her and loved our life together. Work could be stressful at times, but it never outweighed the joy waiting for me at home. We were a team, two people working together to keep the light burning.

The birth of our first daughter Sophie was magical. She arrived two weeks late, and my wife was incredibly brave through the pain. I held her hands, whispered comfort, and tried to steady her through the long hours. She had wanted to avoid pain medication, but eventually, the pain became too much and they gave her something stronger. When our daughter finally came into the world, I was overwhelmed. I held her in my arms, watched her take her first breaths, and felt something shift inside me. It was love in its purest form. Gentle, unconditional, and absolute.

Our second daughter, Julia came into the world through a water birth. It was calmer, easier, and my wife seemed at peace. Again, I was there beside her, the first to hold our child, the one to cut the umbilical cord. Even though I had done it before with Sophie, the feeling was no less miraculous. To hold life like that, to watch it begin. There is nothing else like it.

Family life became the centre of my world. Bath time was one of my favourite moments. The girls would laugh and splash, and I would join in whenever I managed to get home early enough. Later, when they were older, Sundays became our special ritual. I would cook lunch for everyone, often a roast. They would chat and laugh in the kitchen, sometimes helping me peel the potatoes, which they later called "sweeties" because they were small, crispy, and delicious. It was love made visible, the kind that lives in the details.

Some people called us the golden couple, and perhaps for a while we were. There was warmth in our home, laughter in every corner. I supported the girls in everything. School events, drama performances, sports, Christmas carols, parents' evenings, and whatever else was going on. I didn't want to miss a single moment of their childhood. I wanted to be there, to see it all unfold.

There were no signs of what was to come. No slow drift apart. Our marriage had felt whole right up to the moment it wasn't. Then, without warning, Vivian left. She took our daughters with her, and everything that had been our life disappeared overnight. There was no conversation, no response to my plea for help, not even the chance to ask why. I suggested family therapy, but she refused. It was sudden, brutal, and complete.

I still remember her words: "I'm young enough to start again." She said it and grinned with glee at the same time as she saw me suffering, as if the years we had built together were nothing but a chapter she could close at will. That look, that indifference, cut through me in a way I can't describe. She had never shown me that side of herself before. One minute I was in heaven, the next I was in hell. It was like watching my whole world vanish behind a locked door.

I had suffered from depression before, but whatever I carried then, I kept hidden. The illness came later, after the silence, after the absence of my children.

Looking back now, those years were the happiest of my life. Pure, golden, and full of love. But even the smallest shadow can sometimes swallow all the light.

CHAPTER 5

The Shadow of a Father

My father was a man whose presence filled a room even when he said very little. Success surrounded him like a tailored suit. Visible, precise and perfectly pressed. But it never touched those of us who lived inside his orbit. Other men admired him and in some ways feared him: decisive, articulate, confident of his place in the world. To me he was a mystery, a shape that passed through the house leaving faint traces of aftershave and authority, but no warmth.

He was almost always away. When he was home, the sound of his briefcase on the table and the smell of whisky announced him more than any words. He was a chronic alcoholic. My mother would speak of his meetings and the companies that relied on him. I never doubted his talent, only his capacity to be present.

What I remember most is the hush that followed his arrival. The way conversation softened, the air tightening. My sister and I learned early how to fade into the background.

He was sometimes cruel. His precision could slice more cleanly than anger. He expected excellence but never defined it, and praise was foreign to him. Children, to his mind, were something you raised and fed until they proved useful. The small details of our lives, such as who our friends were, didn't register.

Now and then we shared a few minutes in the same space, but I could never quite reach him. His focus was always elsewhere. On business, on headlines, or on the steady refill of his glass. The house showed his success. The houses, the cars, the invitations, the tailored suits, but it did not feel like home. It was more like a showroom of achievement, polished and cold.

As I grew older, the admiration I once felt thinned into something quieter. You cannot resent someone you do not really know; you simply stop expecting anything of them. The silence between us became predictable, almost orderly.

One memory stays with me. I must have been about 10. I had spent the day building a model airplane, the sort of project a boy gives his full heart to. When he came in that night, I waited at the bottom of the stairs, holding it out as proof that I existed. He paused, looked at it, and said:

"You'll make a mess if you keep using that glue indoors." Then he walked past. I stood there, the plane in my hands, feeling the air shift as he went by. It was a relatively small thing, but it told me everything.

He was, in every sense, a distant figure. At first it was geography. Flights, meetings and dinners, but distance soon became habit. By the time I was old enough to want conversation, the silence had hardened. We never argued because there was nothing to argue about. He lived sealed inside his own success.

When I experienced my first breakdown years later, the manic rush that sent me spiralling towards Heathrow, it was him I was reaching for. Somewhere in the confusion, I was still that boy with the model plane, desperate for his acknowledgement and attention. I wanted to tell him I loved him, and to hear those words back. Of course, he never did, and he wasn't there; he never had been, and never would be. That absence became the thread running through everything that followed.

My mother was different. She had warmth, a quick empathy that softened the sharp edges of our home. When she was around, the air felt easier to breathe.

Years later, when I held my first child, the past returned in sudden clarity. I understood, without words, what my father had failed to give and what I must offer in its place. I remember thinking, I will not be him. There was no vow, only a quiet decision to show up. To be present. To know the small things that matter to a child. Their fears, their jokes, and their ordinary days.

I turned down very prestigious jobs that would have taken me abroad. Friends called it short-sighted. They said success demanded sacrifice. But I had lived the cost of that creed. I chose differently. I stayed in Sussex, close to my daughters. I helped with homework, went to school concerts, watched films on the sofa with them and the dogs curled at our feet. Those small, ordinary moments healed something in me. They stitched a tear I had carried since childhood.

I still made it to the Board of Directors by the age of 38, despite some occasions when I had no income at all. This proves that mental illness can challenge you, but it doesn't have to define your limits. With persistence, patience, and determination, it is possible to push through and reach your potential, however big or small.

Sometimes I wonder if my father ever saw the distance between us, if he understood what he and I had both missed. Perhaps he believed his way of love was providing, achieving, and maintaining order. Perhaps he never noticed the silence at all. He is long gone now, and the questions no longer burn.

He was a product of his time, shaped by lessons that made tenderness seem weak. Knowing that doesn't erase the hurt, but it explains it. I have always been a caring person, but in some strange symmetry his absence became my teacher. It taught me to be present, to listen, to reach for my children instead of away from them.

When I picture him now, he's standing on a railway platform, briefcase in hand, the train gathering speed. I'm a boy on the other side of the glass, waving. He nods once, distracted, already elsewhere. The train moves on, and he disappears into his own distance. Yet even now, his shadow lingers. Not as a curse, but as a compass, pointing me toward the father I chose to become.

CHAPTER 6

The Bipolar Battle

I have faced 3 major episodes of mania. The first occurred during university, when I was 20. It arrived without warning, sweeping me into a world I barely recognised. One moment I was steady and grounded, and the next, my thoughts raced far ahead of reality. Emotions spilled faster than I could contain, sleep became irrelevant, and my senses got intense. The world felt both thrilling and uncontrollable. At first, it was intoxicating. But within weeks, the highs collapsed. The fall was harsh. Days slipped away, and confidence shattered. I was left disoriented and ashamed. That episode taught me that control is fragile, and that recovery is ongoing work.

The second episode came years later, once I had established more stability. Work, a home, and routines I had carefully built. The manic surge was shorter, less intense, yet it carried a depression that ran deeper and lasted far longer than the mania itself. Recovery demanded deliberate effort and a careful rebuilding, step by step.

The third episode was the most complicated, not only because of the illness but because it was triggered by the deepest personal loss I have ever faced. My oldest daughter Sophie 'ghosted' me completely, from one day to the next. She stopped all contact of any kind with me, without ever explaining why, even to this day.

Her absence carved a wound into my life that created an unbearable depression, even by my standards. It lasted for 3 years with terrible symptoms. This episode demanded more than just recovery; it required piecing my life back together while carrying the weight of grief that had no easy resolution.

Depression has always been a persistent companion. There are days when the world loses its meaning. Those days remind me that mental illness is often quiet and stealthy, yet its impact is enduring, and still, life can continue. The illness interrupts, but it has never completely erased my drive to keep going.

Despite all this, as I mentioned before, I have managed to have a very successful career, having kept my mental health problems private from my employers. Because of the stigma, I guarantee that if I had disclosed anything at all, I would have lost my job, and my prospects of finding another position would have been minimal.

Every time I faced a serious episode, I focused on doing what I could to survive and rebuild. I took medication reluctantly, because I have always resisted pills, but they helped me get past the worst moments. Therapy was a significant help at times. A space to speak without judgment, to untangle thoughts, and to begin rebuilding life one step at a time. Recovery has never been instant. It is deliberate and patient, measured in small acts like keeping routines, attending therapy, and noticing early signs of struggle. Later, I will share some 'Top Tips' which I used to good effect.

Through this process, awareness became a vital tool. It is not a cure, but it has given me a sense of control I did not have before. The illness has never defined me. Episodes, particularly depressive ones, have been enduring teachers, showing me patience and the limits of control.

These lessons have shaped how I face the hardest losses, including losing contact with my children, which is the pain I feel most sharply, because Julia followed her sister's example, but much later when she was 20. Their absence feeds the depression, reminding me that recovery is not linear. Yet at the same time, it reinforces the importance of presence and showing up, even when life feels uncertain. Life is imperfect, but it is the ordinary moments, the small, everyday acts, that matter most.

Over time, my approach shifted from fighting bipolar disorder as an enemy to understanding it as a condition I needed to work with. Awareness, therapy, medication, and self-care became tools to maintain stability and some form of quality of life. Each day offered a chance to reinforce these practices and honour the life I had built.

The illness was part of the story, not the headline. Resilience was not about grand gestures, but the quiet act of getting up when exhaustion tempted surrender, and it was persistence, not perfection, that sustained a life worth living.

I live with that balance in mind. Highs, lows, heartbreak, and simple joys all belong to my story. I do not chase manic peaks, nor fear depressive lows more than I need to. I have rebuilt repeatedly, each time stronger and wiser. The illness is a chapter, not the whole story. One day at a time, one deliberate act at a time. In the quiet, ordinary moments of most days, I find the truest testament to life's strength and meaning.

CHAPTER 7

Parental Alienation

Parental alienation is a topic so painful that it demands its own focus. I discovered it the hard way, and it shook the foundations of everything I thought I knew about love, trust, and family. I never expected that my own mental health would be turned into a weapon against me, used to manipulate my children and destroy my place in their lives.

As my daughters grew, it became increasingly clear that they were being influenced to see me as a bad father. There is an official name for this now, Parental Alienation, which has only been truly recognised in the last 5 years or so, and the label is painfully appropriate. When my children abandoned me, the shock was absolute. I had a crushing realisation that the alienation had worked extremely well.

Of course, no parent is perfect, but I know myself, and the friends and family around me would agree, that I have always been a present and doting father. I made sacrifices for my children, turning down glamorous work abroad to ensure my weekends revolved entirely around them. My diary, my time, and my energy were always theirs. Every effort I made was to be the father they deserved, and yet that seemed to count for nothing in the eyes of the other side.

The alienation was aggravated by my mental health. I wrote countless letters trying to calm the situation, to remind my ex-wife that children should never be caught in parental conflict. That they needed a father's input as much a mother's. I failed every time. I did not threaten legal action, because I hoped it could be resolved calmly. Once, I had no choice but to take her to court because she interfered with my contact, cancelling visits at very short notice without explanation. That moment brought the most concrete evidence of the betrayal.

The Headmistress of my daughters' school, Mrs. Light, wrote a statement that shocked me to my core ***(See Appendix on page 71 for the official statement)***. She described how my ex-wife's mother, the children's grandmother, had spoken in front of Julia, calling me a *"disgusting man, who is bipolar and not fit to be in charge of children."* It was said in full hearing of Julia, and it was clear to the staff that they bore considerable hostility towards me. As I said, there are countless other examples. The letters I wrote, brief meetings where behaviour was atrocious, but I will not include them here, as there are simply too many. The statement alone, however, was sufficient to show the betrayal I had long suspected, and it was heavy. Years later, when Julia was 22, she was asked by one of my friends, without my knowing, if he could talk to her. Her response was incredible: "you'll have to check with my Mum". At that age, I think most people make decisions for themselves. I certainly did, and I know my friends did also. A straight "yes" or a "no" would have sufficed, but her response showed clearly that her mother was still in complete control. And please remember, this was a question about speaking to one of my friends, not me.

Parental alienation of this sort is devastating, yet so common. It is almost impossible to prevent if one parent is determined to isolate the children. Fathers sometimes indulge in it as well, but I never did. In retrospect, I was naive. Writing letters had no impact. Going to court was expensive, nearly impossible for some, but the idea of losing my children was far too powerful to stop me.

This personal betrayal also connects to a wider truth about mental health stigma. Society still misunderstands conditions like bipolar disorder, and in some ways, it is weaponised in the same way other identities were decades ago. Words like "*bipolar*" are still loaded with judgement, shame, and above all a complete lack of understanding.

I know only too well the isolation that comes with it. Even now, there is some lingering sense of embarrassment. The manic phases for me are brief, only a couple of weeks at a time, while depression is the crushing part, sapping the will to continue.

I cannot help but think of the LGBTQIA+ community and how it must have felt to be forced into silence decades ago. Through strength and perseverance, much has changed for them. That is part of why I wrote this book. I want mental health to reach that point too, where people do not have to hide, where they do not feel excommunicated or isolated because of who they are or the struggles they carry.

The first abandonment, when Sophie stopped all contact, triggered a manic depressive episode that was extremely severe. It is worth noting that the letter telling me not to contact her did not come directly from her, but from her mother – more evidence of who was really in control.

The depression after the 2 week mania lasted 3 entire years. I often spent 3 days at a time unable to move (literally!), not even to open my eyes or mouth. I was immobilised by grief. My girlfriend at the time supported me as best she could, and I remain deeply grateful for her attention and love. Doctors could not find a physical cause. I now know it was entirely linked to the trauma of my eldest daughter ghosting me.

The second loss, Julia's abandonment, destroyed me again, although without the physical immobility. The depression has remained frequent and severe since then. Suicidal thoughts, and even planning it, have been a recurring presence over the years.

There have been no small victories with my children. I have endured, survived, and tried every technique I could to maintain connection, but they have been blocked from reaching me, and I have had to accept that. Resilience has been my only recourse. Helping others with similar struggles has become a channel for my love and hope.

The contrast between those early years of happiness and this chapter of betrayal could not have been more profound. I had loved meeting my ex-wife, the magic of our wedding, the births of Sophie and Julia, the laughter that filled our home, the holidays, the quiet routines that made family life so rich. And then, overnight, it all vanished. My children, who had once been the centre of my world, became a complete enigma. The absence was deafening, the silence unrelenting, and the lack of explanation only deepened the heartbreak. Every memory of joy now carried a sharp edge, a reminder of what had been lost without warning or reason.

I do believe that, in some way, my children still love me, but they are unable to communicate, and the channels that should exist have been blocked. My belief in true love has been deeply shaken. Trust in others has been eroded. People can say one thing and then do another. Yet, despite the devastation, resilience has carried me forward. That quiet persistence is what allows me to continue, to survive, and to channel my love into the world in ways that might make a difference.

This chapter is a testimony to Parental Alienation, to the impact of misunderstanding mental health, and to the enduring challenge of love when it is obstructed by others. It is a chapter of sorrow, of betrayal, and of survival. It is a chapter of the 5% of life that can overwhelm the 95%, and a reminder that even when everything falls away, the will to endure, to show up, and to love remains the most powerful act of all.

CHAPTER 8

An Extreme Manifestation of Trauma

There comes a moment when the mind can no longer hold what it has been carrying, and the body is forced to speak instead. Mine did not whisper. It collapsed. It folded inward under the weight of everything I had been carrying in silence.

It started 2 weeks after I received the letter from Mrs. Vivian Burns (my ex-wife). It came via email. The contents were crushing. I felt a mix of confusion and later hope because I tried to tell myself it might be temporary, that things could still change. I read the words several times, slowly, trying to make sense of them.

Then my eyes stopped on the line that carried everything: "for the foreseeable future."

I read those four words, letting them sink in slowly. At first, they felt like part of a formal letter, something distant and official. But the weight of them settled into me, undeniable and heavy, pressing down with a quiet certainty I could not ignore. For a while, I tried to act as if it was just a difficult moment. I reached out to Sophie on WhatsApp, keeping some form of contact alive, hoping that the distance might soften, that things could change.

Weeks later, another message arrived from Mrs. Burns, this time leaving no room for hope. It told me to stop all contact completely. There was no explanation, no attempt at compassion, just finality. I read that message multiple times, as if going over the words again might make them less real. It didn't. Each reading only confirmed the truth I was struggling to accept: the last thread of connection had been cut.

At first, I clung to hope. I told myself that Sophie was still under influence, being manipulated, that the bond we had shared might somehow be restored. But as days bled into weeks, weeks stretched into months, and months turned into years. It dawned on me that the brainwashing had worked so well that Sophie herself had finally been convinced into this frame of mind.

The hope I had clung to began to fracture, then collapse, and with it came a suffering I had never known before. It solidified like a wall between us. And slowly, it dawned on me that I might never hear from her again, might never see her again. And to this day, I still haven't.

That is when my body completely broke down. It was as if every part of me had decided that continuing was impossible. My mind still refused to fully accept it, but my body could no longer wait and it collapsed under the grief I could not escape.

It felt as though my body was sending me a message to give up. I could not move. It was beyond extreme. It was the worst kind of malignant depression anyone had ever seen.

Doctors examined me and referred me to many specialists. I underwent repeated tests and scans: blood work, neurological assessments, and other investigations. But nothing abnormal was found. No clear explanation was ever given.

During this period, the thoughts began. They did not arrive dramatically. They crept in quietly, like a logical conclusion to unbearable pain. At first, they were just passing shadows. Then they became conversations I had with myself. Then they became plans. I reached the second stage of the suicide pyramid: first the thoughts, then the planning. The third and fourth are attempting suicide, and then finally, succeeding.

I have never attempted suicide, but have planned it a thousand times. Doctors normally intervene at this stage because of the Hippocratic oath, but I hid it. Shame lived alongside fear. And truthfully, neither the medications nor the talk therapy I had tried before ever touched the depths of what I was living through.

This time, I experienced mania which lasted nearly a month, the longest of the 3 episodes. It began at my mother's house. My girlfriend was there, and they both noticed the change in me. During that phase, I felt extremely strong, as if nothing could touch me. But over time, the mania became unhinged.

I remember a distinct moment of desperation. I knelt on the ground before my mother and begged her to give me her gun. I knew she had one somewhere, though I wasn't sure if it was still in the house. Of course, she never gave it to me, thank goodness.

That was when they called an ambulance. I was taken to the hospital and sectioned. I had no idea what was happening at the time. There was a security guard outside my door 24 hours a day, to make sure I did not harm myself, or try to escape.

At the time, I had no understanding of what was happening or how serious it was. Only later did I understand how close I had come to truly harming myself, and I knew the guards outside my hospital door were there because the mania had carried me to a place where I could no longer be trusted with my own life.

Something bizarre happened. I tried to pray to Allah, and I'm not even religious. I have never practised Islam. I tried to face Mecca, though I wasn't even sure of the correct direction, and sang prayers I did not know, in a language I could not speak. I do not speak a word of Arabic. It was gibberish. I have no idea why I did it. It was just a very small part of the manic phase.

Part 2

The Seeds of Hope

CHAPTER 9

From Pain to Purpose

When Covid first struck, I happened to be in Cape Town, South Africa. The government relaxed all Visa requirements, so I was able to stay for nearly 2 years. During that time, I read an article in the Guardian newspaper online, which shocked me to my core. I then went about the rest of my day in a normal fashion, and went to bed without thinking about the article.

I woke up the next morning with an idea fully formed in my mind. It simply arrived, as if the night had done all the hard work and left me with a single, clear thought: I had to create a charity. The clarity was staggering. It was as though my own suffering, the storms I had survived, the grief I carried from my daughters, and the years of seeing others struggle, had all condensed into this singular purpose. Pain had turned itself into possibility, grief into action.

The Guardian piece had reported the results of a massive survey conducted by University College London, supported by the Royal College of Psychiatrists' Child & Adolescent Faculty, among others. The survey focused on 19,000 young people, and they were able to analyse specifically 17 year olds. I remember the numbers as though they had branded themselves into my mind. 25 percent, so 1 in 4, had self-harmed in the last 12 months. 7 percent had attempted suicide at some point in their lives. I know firsthand that the numbers have got significantly worse since Covid, because a South African organisation called SADAG (South African Depression and Anxiety Group) which is similar to the Samaritans in the UK, and the largest organisation of that type in the whole of Africa, started to receive 3 times as many calls in a very short space of time.

All these statistics shocked me. They were not just numbers. They were warnings, cries for help embedded in research, and yet they felt under-reported and understated. I knew there were many more who had not shared, who would never admit their hardships because of the shame and stigma surrounding mental health. And I understood that better than most. I had never carried out an attempt, but I had planned suicide thousands of times, quite literally. I had lived with those thoughts circling in my mind, tightening their grip during my darkest moments. That experience gave me empathy, a deep, almost tangible understanding of what these people were facing. Most people would have closed the article and moved on. I could not.

I had no step-by-step plan, no funding, yet the need and clarity were undeniable. My struggles, my experience, and my empathy demanded that I act.

I sat down immediately and began working on a business plan. I wrote with feverish focus, sketching out how the charity could function, how it could reach the ones in need, how it could prevent self-harm and support mental health. I shared it with a few people whose opinions I trusted, taking in their feedback and refining the plan. And then I made a decision that shocked even me. I would launch it myself. I would not wait for a year or 2 to seek outside funding. The sums involved were enormous by my standards. It was a massive financial commitment. But the desire to act, to prevent the difficulties, was stronger than any hesitation. I simply could not put it off.

2 months later, Hope Guardians was officially launched using my own money. That is fast by any standards for a start-up. I could not delay, given the urgency of the problem. From the moment I decided to act, everything was focused on making the charity real and functional. The decision was swift, almost rash, but the desire to prevent misery and turn my pain into purpose was stronger than any hesitation.

Looking back, I see now how irrational some might have thought my decision. I was risking not just my finances, but the quiet stability I had fought to build after years of struggle. Every penny I used, every commitment I made, carried weight. Yet rationality did not matter that morning. Purpose mattered. Action mattered. And for the first time in my life, I felt the full force of turning personal pain into public good.

It was not easy. Even after the launch, the challenge of raising funds became immediate and unavoidable. I have never been naturally adept at asking for help. My strengths lie in business, in entrepreneurship, in generating value and creating solutions. Making money for myself or a company came naturally.

Asking for donations, even for something that was not about me, did not. I knew that Hope Guardians required the support of a community willing to believe in the mission alongside me. My own attempts to raise money have largely failed, I am ashamed to admit.

Writing this book, in part, is an extension of that work. It is an invitation. Not for my benefit, but for the adolescents, the ones who struggle in silence, who face stigma, who battle mental health crises every single day. By sharing this story, by revealing the numbers, the urgency, and the emotional truth behind Hope Guardians. Through this platform, I aim to open doors for support, engagement, and funding. Every word is meant to bridge the gap between awareness and action, to transform empathy into real support.

From the moment I made that decision, every action, every step of the launch, was focused on turning the fully formed idea into a real, functioning charity. The execution demanded courage and persistence, but the purpose behind it, the chance to prevent torment and support those in crisis, created its own momentum, pushing me forward even when the challenge felt immense.

That first morning of clarity stayed with me. It marked the beginning of *Hope Guardians.* It constantly reminds me that even from the darkest experiences, purpose can emerge, and that one person's choice to act, fully and without hesitation, can create change.

CHAPTER 10

The Business Model: copy away!

The strength of Hope Guardians does not come from complexity. It comes from efficiency. The model behind the organisation is intentionally simple, but it contains one crucial innovative element that makes it uniquely powerful, which is the ability to deliver large volumes of therapy at an extremely low average cost. This simplicity is what makes the model effective, and it is also what gives it the potential to scale globally.

The ambition was never to build something small or local. From the beginning, the vision was to create a structure so efficient and adaptable that it could be replicated across countries, regions, and cities. An extremely lean model that could grow without becoming bloated. A framework that could serve thousands, then millions, especially if it is replicated by others.

At the centre of this model are 4 clear pillars. Each one is essential. Each one supports the others. Without any one of them, the structure would collapse.

Recruiting Therapists: The Engine of the Model

The most important pillar of Hope Guardians is the recruitment of therapists.

There is a very clear reason for this. Therapists are the engine of the organisation. Without them, nothing else matters. No marketing, no funding, no visibility can replace the presence of qualified, compassionate professionals willing to give their time.

The system does not rely on traditional mass employment. Instead, therapists who work for Hope Guardians go into their own professional networks and ask for 1 free hour per week of their time. 1 single hour.

Before launching the organisation, I tested this theory myself. I needed proof that it would work. Over 90% of professionals said "yes". That figure still astonishes me. It is a testament to the nature of the people who enter this profession. To work in mental health you have to be deeply caring. You have to want to help people. You do not choose this work for glory.

Because of that, every time a new therapist joins, I feel genuine gratitude. Each one represents a young life that might not be lost to silence.

The structure grows through connection. These therapists then go back into their own networks and recruit more therapists. Those therapists recruit others, and so on. The network expands organically. With hundreds, even thousands, of therapists come thousands of free therapy sessions for those who may otherwise have no access to help at all.

In some ways, it is similar to the old-fashioned "pyramid" marketing idea, but obviously we are not selling a product, we are asking for help.

The number one operational priority for Hope Guardians is to expand this internal therapist network. This allows growth to be exponential and reduces the cost per session even further, increasing both reach and sustainability.

Safety remains non-negotiable. To protect the people we serve, every therapist is required to provide proof of qualifications, proof of membership of their regulatory body, and proof of professional insurance.

Beyond therapy itself, Hope Guardians' employed professionals also play a critical role in matching people to the right 'external' therapists. This careful matching process improves outcomes, builds trust, and ensures that each young person feels seen and understood.

All services are delivered online. This serves two crucial purposes: safety, and cost reduction. Online delivery lowers risk, removes unnecessary physical vulnerabilities, and dramatically reduces operational costs. This allows the organisation to scale more effectively and reach more people rather than sinking resources into physical infrastructure.

The model is so streamlined that it can be reproduced. Anyone could create a similar initiative in their own country, region, or city. Starting small with a freelance structure, just as I did, and slowly growing it over time. This, I believe, is how millions of people can be helped, not by one organisation alone, but through replication of a proven model. So please, feel free to copy away!

I am willing to offer guidance to anyone who wishes to do this. Freely, without charge.

Hope Guardians will continue to grow. But the global need is too vast for any single organisation to solve alone. With approximately 1 billion individuals worldwide in need of mental health support, global scaling of this model is not just an ambition, it is a necessity.

Donating: Financial Support as a Foundation

The second pillar of Hope Guardians is funding. Donations, Corporate Sponsorships, and financial contributions of all kinds are essential to the survival and expansion of the organisation. Thanks to the volunteer-based therapist network, operational overheads are minimal, meaning that every pound contributed goes further. Even so, there are vital systems that require resources: coordination, safeguarding, technology, and safety procedures all rely on financial support to function effectively.

Just as the organisation depends on the generosity of therapists, it also relies on the generosity of supporters who believe in the mission.

Ideally, a specialist fundraiser could be employed, someone capable enough to raise funds not only to cover their own salary, but to contribute significantly beyond that. The reality is that individuals of that calibre are rare, and they come at a cost. Even so, anyone who feels they can genuinely support this work is encouraged to get in touch at: hello@hopeguardians.com

Fighting the Stigma: Recognising some Mental Health issues as Deadly Diseases

The third pillar is the active fight against mental health stigma. For many, mental health is not a minor issue. It is a deadly disease. In the United Kingdom alone, there are approximately 1.3 million people, around 2 percent of the population who suffer from Bipolar Disorder alone. The figure may not be perfect, but it highlights the sheer scale of the problem.

Some people claim that stigma no longer exists. I know that is not true. From my point of view, I still feel extremely vulnerable when I talk about my own struggles. I do not give the full details, because I am ashamed to admit it. Writing this book has been difficult precisely because it exposes parts of me that my friends and family never knew existed. It is made even more poignant by the fact that I am susceptible to depression if this very important mission fails.

Younger generations are thankfully more open, more willing to talk. The LGBTQIA+ community, in particular, has broken many social barriers through courage and visibility. Mental health, however, remains decades behind. The silence still lingers, and the fear of judgement remains real.

Changing this culture is not optional. It is essential. Treating mental health with the seriousness it deserves, recognising its potential to be life-threatening, and actively challenging stigma is central to the mission of Hope Guardians.

Talking: Creating a Culture of Honesty

The fourth pillar is conversation. Talking openly. Encouraging dialogue. Creating space for honesty.

I have sometimes been called "the ice breaker" because I cannot explain why Hope Guardians exists without revealing my own struggles. What happens next is astonishing, and always the same. When one person opens up, others follow. People begin sharing their own stories, their own burdens, their own fears, or sometimes the struggles of people in their network of friends/family/ colleagues/etc.

Once, a conversation shifted my perspective entirely. I had been discussing how many people suffer from mental health conditions, or at least know someone who does. Someone suggested I was asking the wrong question. Not *"How many people suffer?"* but *"How many people do not?"* The answer, of course, is that very few are untouched.

This pillar is about creating space for those conversations. Giving people permission to speak without shame. Building environments where silence is no longer the default, and honesty becomes part of the culture.

Efficiency, Scale, and the Global Vision

All four pillars exist to serve a single purpose: to reach those in need, to provide support when it matters most, and to create lasting impact. This is not just about running a charity. It is about building a framework capable of growth, adaptation, and replication. Hope Guardians is designed to expand beyond borders, to inspire similar initiatives worldwide, and to ensure that help is never out of reach. It is a model built to endure, a blueprint for hope that can be shared, multiplied, and improved, creating a global movement that puts those who struggle first.

CHAPTER 11

A Message to Sufferers

To anyone reading this who is trapped in silence, I want you to know one thing clearly: mental health is not a death sentence. Bipolar disorder, depression, anxiety, or any serious condition does not define the limits of your life. It is a chapter, not the whole story. Hope is not just a word, it is the key. It is the single most important indicator of your quality of life, and it is what allows survival even when the darkness feels all-encompassing.

This chapter is for those who are suffering, yes, but it is also for the people quietly helping them. Friends, family, carers; your kindness matters more than you realise. Even a single word of encouragement, a presence that listens without judgment, a reference to the 'Top Tips', can be a lifeline. And if you are one of those people offering support, know that what you are doing is seen, felt, and deeply needed.

I speak from experience. 30 years of struggling with serious depression, countless moments when the thought of giving up felt like the only escape, have shown me that nothing lasts forever. Pain, even the deepest and most exhausting kind, eventually shifts. That understanding became the lifeline I held on to. It kept me alive long enough to see change. And that is why this book is named *Hope: A Blueprint for Healing*, because hope is not a vague idea. It is a tool, a direction, something you can return to when everything else feels like it is falling apart.

This is where our work at Hope Guardians becomes crucial. When we help someone through Hope Guardians, we think in terms of a scale. Picture life as a scale from 0 to 10: 0 is unbearable, where the thought of continuing is literally impossible. 10 is fully living, a state we might never stay at permanently, but one we aim to approach. Someone at 0 is often contemplating suicide, unable to see light or feel joy. Our goal, step by step, is to get them to 5. That is a meaningful improvement. They start to socialise again, take small steps back into normal life, begin to eat properly, sleep more regularly, regain confidence, and rebuild a sense of belonging. Reaching 5 is not full recovery, but it is a turning point.

From there, the aim is to climb toward 8 or 9. Sustainable stability, where joy, purpose, and hope co-exist. This takes time. It takes courage. It takes commitment from the person themselves and from those supporting them. Every hour of therapy, every small victory, every gentle encouragement counts. When we succeed, we are not just improving days, we are saving lives. A life cannot always be lived at a 10, but restoring hope and giving a person the tools to live fully again is just as valuable.

If you are reading this, and you are at your lowest, it may feel impossible to start. Even the simplest acts can seem monumental. That is why I want to offer some practical guidance. Steps you can begin with, at your own pace. You do not need to do everything at once. Pick 1 or 2, and start there. Even tiny actions can begin the road to recovery. These aren't rules. They're simply steps that have helped countless people, including me. You can obviously Google/ Chat GPT/other your specific requirements, and start from there.

1. Gentle Lifestyle Habits

These are the foundations. They seem simple, but simplicity matters when the mind is heavy.

- **Move your body daily**: Even a 20 minute walk can release endorphins and regulate stress hormones. Outdoors is best. Sunlight, fresh air, and a brief change of scenery matter. You do not need to run a marathon. Small, consistent movement is enough to start shifting your energy.
- **Eat regularly and nutritiously**: Blood sugar stability affects mood far more than we often realise. Aim for whole foods, fruit, protein, and plenty of water. Avoid caffeine after 4pm; it may seem trivial, but it can affect sleep and overall balance.
- **Sleep hygiene**: Try to keep a consistent bedtime and wake time, even on weekends. Avoid screens in the hour before bed. If you cannot sleep, do not force it. Get out of bed after 20 minutes, do

something calming, and return when ready. This is hard, but it matters.

- **Reduce alcohol and stimulants**: They may numb temporarily, but over time they deepen depression. Every small reduction helps.

2. Reconnection and Routine

Depression thrives in isolation. Building structure and connection matters:

- **Small daily structure**: Plan gentle routines: meals, a short walk, one pleasant task. Even minor stability begins to retrain the mind.
- **Social contact**: Speak to someone daily, even briefly. Chat with a barista, say hello to a neighbour, join a small local group. Connection is medicine.
- **Volunteer or join a group**: Purpose and belonging are powerful antidotes to emptiness. Start with something manageable, even a single hour per week.

3. Mental and Emotional Skills

How you relate to your thoughts shapes your experience:

- **Cognitive reframing**: Challenge "always" or "never" thoughts. Ask yourself: "What is another way to view this?" Small shifts in perspective reduce the power of negativity.
- **Mindfulness or meditation**: Grounding in the present moment diminishes rumination. Apps

like Headspace, Calm, or Insight Timer help. It is a skill that takes practice, but persistence pays off.

- **Self-compassion**: Treat yourself as you would a dear friend. Harsh self-criticism only deepens despair. You are not at fault for your suffering. Healing takes time, and that is okay.

4. Professional Help

Serious support matters, and seeking it is not weakness.

- **Therapy**: Cognitive Behavioural Therapy (CBT), Acceptance and Commitment Therapy (ACT), or interpersonal therapy, among others, are effective. Hope Guardians focuses on supporting those without other options. If you cannot afford therapy or are blocked by other systems, reach out.
- **Medication**: For moderate to severe depression, antidepressants can rebalance brain chemistry. Discuss with a GP or Psychiatrist. This is not failure, it is a tool to get you back on track.
- **Support groups**: Sharing with people who understand your experience reduces isolation. Hearing "I get it" is profound.

5. Meaning and Enjoyment

Depression often drains colour from life, but pleasure can be rebuilt:

- **Do something small you used to enjoy**: Even if it feels flat initially. Enjoyment often returns slowly.
- **Spend time in nature**: Sunlight, greenery, and fresh air calm the nervous system and lift mood.
- **Creative expression**: Music, art, journaling; these outlets help release feelings words cannot contain.

I know these steps are hard, especially at the lowest points. But hope is not built in one leap; it grows in tiny, steady acts. Each small movement, each step forward, compounds. You may not feel it immediately, but over weeks and months, life can begin to feel bearable, even enjoyable again.

Hope works through action. It grows through small, consistent choices. It is the daily choice to reach for light, to take small steps, to accept help. It is the knowledge that pain, however deep, will pass. It is the courage to keep showing up, even when despair whispers that nothing will change.

If you are helping someone else, your presence is equally vital. Sit with them, listen, hold space without judgment. Even when it feels small, your support is a lifeline. It is proof that connection matters, that people are not alone in their struggle.

You will not reach 10 every day, no one does, and that is okay. Recovery is rarely perfect. But moving from 0 toward 5, then 6, then 7, is huge progress. And progress, however gradual, is life-saving. It is the essence of what

Hope Guardians exists to do: restore hope and rebuild lives, and remind people that they are not defined by their illness. Life can be lived fully again. Sometimes quietly, and sometimes boldly, but always moving forward.

CHAPTER 12

A Message to Givers

Running Hope Guardians has been a personal commitment from the very start. Every pound I have contributed has gone directly into expanding the network of therapists, maintaining safeguarding systems, allowing us to reach those who would otherwise have no access to help at all. This work has tangible impact. As one powerful example, we have so far saved approximately **795 lives** ... sustaining this requires more than my own resources.

Even modest support can transform lives. Imagine the price of a cup of coffee in London, roughly £5. Contributions of this size, when pooled, allow us to mobilise more therapists, strengthen safeguarding systems, and connect young people who feel completely alone with someone who listens, understands, and guides them toward hope.

I think it is important to state that a 1 hour consultation with a Psychiatrist which normally costs about £600 in London, can be delivered by Hope guardians for just £20 because of the business model/pyramid. That is only just over **3%**. That is how lean we are.

But the truth is simple: we are running out of money. Personal funding has sustained us so far, almost exclusively from me, but to continue and expand our work, support from others is essential. Corporate sponsorship could be transformative, enabling wider reach, more ambitious planning, and stronger, resilient systems for those in need.

In practical terms, your support ensures that no teenager reaches a point of complete isolation without access to someone trained to guide them, listen to them, and offer hope. That alone justifies every effort we make to connect people to the cause. The act of giving is not measured by the amount alone but by the change it enables.

This is the reality of being a Founder committed to a cause that is urgent, ongoing, and too important to delay. The generosity of others allows Hope Guardians to exist beyond 1 person.

If you are able to contribute, even at a modest level, please consider doing so via our website, www.hopeguardians.com, by clicking "**Donate**." Each contribution strengthens the network and ensures a young person has someone to reach out to when they need help.

Your support is not just a donation. It is the bridge between despair and hope, isolation and connection, silence and being heard. Every contribution strengthens the organisation.

In a world where too many suffer quietly, your choice to act matters. By giving, you are helping transform small amounts into enormous outcomes, ensuring that Hope Guardians can continue to fulfil its mission and touch the lives of thousands more in need.

The need is real, immediate, and urgent. Hope Guardians has reached this point because of dedication, but it can only move forward with the collective support of individuals and organisations who understand what is at stake.

I invite you to consider taking part, contributing what you can, and helping to ensure that no person has to navigate mental health struggles without support.

CHAPTER 13

A Message to Aspiring Guardians

If you have ever felt a pull to make a difference, to bring hope to young people suffering in silence and isolation, then I want to speak directly to you. The ability to help is not limited by wealth or status. Every one of us can make a meaningful impact, and I am here to show you that it is possible.

The mission I have undertaken with Hope Guardians is not simply a job. It's a calling. Above all, it is the guidance I offer to others that defines this work. I provide it freely, to anyone willing to start their own mission, without expectation or cost. This is not charity or obligation, it is a responsibility I embrace wholeheartedly.

For those who may feel hesitant, unsure of where to begin, I want to reassure you: starting small is enough. You do not need a fortune or vast resources. Even a single committed hour, a modest effort, can spark change. I have witnessed firsthand how small beginnings ripple outward, touching more lives than anyone could predict. And for those fortunate enough to have more substantial means, it is possible to delegate operational responsibilities to a Managing Director, ensuring your initiative grows efficiently while staying true to its purpose. To repeat, guidance from me is freely available to all. No cost, no expectation; simply a shared commitment to doing what is right.

Imagine hundreds, or even thousands, of people reading these words and feeling the drive to act. That is the vision I hold. I am convinced that action, rooted in genuine care, can transform despair into hope, loneliness into connection, and silence into conversation. You can make all the difference, not because of what you possess, but because of the choice to stand up, to lead, to care.

This is why I offer my knowledge freely. Because I truly believe that I was born to do this. Not for recognition, not for reward, but because it is the mission that aligns with the deepest parts of who I am. It is a way to channel love, empathy, and dedication into something meaningful. Every job I have held pales in comparison to the fulfilment this work brings. It is not simply work; it is purpose, heart, and a responsibility to serve.

So, if you are considering stepping forward, do not wait for permission or perfect conditions. Take the first step, and know that you are not alone. I will walk beside anyone willing to commit to this path, helping you navigate the challenges, celebrate the victories, and ensure that your mission has real impact.

In the end, this is more than an invitation. It is a call to action, a reminder that one person, with care, courage, and determination, can ignite change that spreads far beyond what they can imagine.

Together, we can create a network of hope, and show young people that someone cares, that someone is willing to act, that they are not forgotten.

CHAPTER 14

Conclusion: Unwavering Drive

Looking back, every high and low, every moment of struggle and joy, has shaped who I am today. The empathy that guides my every decision, comes directly from a life that has known deep suffering. Those dark periods, indescribable in their intensity, have left a lasting mark. Pain that at its worst feels all-consuming. And yet, in the wider view of life, it is only a fraction of my story. Painful as it is, this suffering has given me the insight and drive to help others.

The rest of my life, by contrast, has been filled with moments of beauty and joy. For a long time, I thought nothing gave me greater joy than the drive along the Cape Town coast, the 'Twelve Apostles" catching the sunlight, wind on my face, the world stretching endlessly around me. It was breathtaking, and for a time, I believed that was my favourite feeling.

But reflection has a way of revealing truth. No view, no scenic panorama, no fleeting thrill compares to the sheer elation I felt when picking up my children from school. That simple act, driving up to the gates, seeing them run and laugh floods me with a joy I cannot describe. Weather, traffic, or worries vanish in that moment. The mundane transforms into something extraordinary, and I am reminded of why life matters. That feeling, so pure and powerful, is the kind of drive I try to bring into every day, every decision, every effort to help others.

It is this combination of suffering and joy, of hardship and love, that has forged my purpose. I want my pain to mean something. I want it to be a source of light for those who find themselves in the darkest corners of life.

And more than anything, I hope that by sharing my story, by showing what is possible when one chooses to act with care and determination, others will find the courage to do the same.

If even a handful of people reading these words are inspired to step forward, to start their own mission, to make the world a little kinder and a little safer, then every moment of struggle I have endured has been worthwhile. My wish is that no suffering goes unnoticed, that every act of compassion, however small, spreads outward like ripples in water, reaching places we cannot always see but which need it the most.

So, I leave you with this thought: purpose is not found in grand gestures or endless plans. It is found in the moments that make your heart soar, in the acts that lift others. Whether it is holding a child's hand, listening to a person in despair, or creating opportunities for someone to feel seen, these are the moments that define a life of meaning.

My hope is simple. That my life, with all its struggles and joys, serves as an example. That it inspires millions to discover their own purpose and to reach out and help others.

Above all, I believe I was born to do this, and it is my deepest wish that the light I have found in my own children and in my work will ignite something just as beautiful in you.

Life, in all its complexity, is worth every step, every act of love, every moment we dedicate to lifting someone else. And if my story can remind even one person of that truth, then it has achieved its purpose.

Appendix

Statement of Mrs Light

I, Mrs. Light, of "000 Grey Street, London W14 9XX" make this statement believing the same to be true to the best of my knowledge, information and belief and in the knowledge that it will be placed before the Court in these proceedings.

I am the Headmistress of The Prep School. The Applicant and the Respondent came to my attention as a result of their children, Sophie and Julia, being placed as pupils at my school. The children started at The Prep on the first day of the autumn term, namely 8th September 2010.

Both Sophie and Julia appeared as happy, normal children. I taught Sophie personally every week and she did seem very happy and settled.

Obviously, I was made aware by Mrs. Vivian Burns and Mr. Nightingale in separate meetings of the background to the children joining the school and was aware of the difficulties between the parents.

Julia missed a lot of schooling due to illness and this was a cause for concern, as we did not, in my view, get satisfactory medical information from a qualified source as to the reasons for Julia being off school.

In October 2010 I received a letter from Mrs. Vivian Burns notifying me that Sophie and Julia were leaving The Prep School "with immediate effect". I attach a copy of that letter (exhibit JE1). I was very surprised to see the letter. I was even more surprised to see the reasons given for the children leaving. The children did not appear to me to be unhappy and had shown no signs of being unsettled whilst at school, although Mrs. Vivian Burns had e-mailed various members of staff alerting them to the fact that Sophie was stressed. I responded to Mrs. Vivian Burns with a letter dated 22nd October 2010, a copy of which I also attach (exhibit JE2). I was particularly upset for the children as they did not even have the opportunity to say goodbye to the friends they had made at the school. A meeting had been arranged for me to meet with Mrs. Vivian Burns and Mr. Nightingale on 18th October to see how we could help the children and to discuss the concerns I and the school had as to the time the children had had off school. In the event this meeting did not take place as, of course, I received the aforesaid letter from Mrs. Vivian Burns on 15th October.

As I have said, I and the school had been concerned in particular as to the time off school Julia had had and the difficulties experienced with Mrs. Vivian Burns and her mother, in particular, when this issue was raised with them.

Prior to Mrs. Vivian Burns removing the children from the school there was, unfortunately, an unpleasant incident at the school involving Mrs. Vivian Burns and her mother.

Mrs. Vivian Burns and her mother were seeing Julia into her classroom, which is adjacent to Mrs. Bonnie's office.

Mrs. Bonnie is the school's SENCO and Child Protection Officer. In accordance with her duties, Mrs. Bonnie asked Mrs. Vivian Burns for a medical certificate to cover Julia's prolonged absence from school. Mrs. Vivian Burns reacted rather badly to this and I understand burst into tears and accused Mrs. Bonnie of calling her a liar. Unfortunately, Mrs. Vivian Burns's mother then interjected herself and sought to make comments, blaming the whole situation upon Mr. Nightingale, calling him a "disgusting man" and saying that he (meaning Mr. Nightingale) was bipolar and not fit to be in charge of children. This was in the full hearing of Julia. It was clear that Mrs. Vivian Burns's mother appeared to bear considerable ill will towards Mr. Nightingale and, as stated, made her remarks in the full hearing of Julia.

I would point out that Mrs. Bonnie was only fulfilling her duties in asking for a medical certificate. We are required under child protection regulation to obtain a medical certificate for a child's absence when they have been absent from school for five days or more. The reasons for this are obvious. Mrs. Bonnie subsequently contacted the duty officer at Hammersmith & The Prep School social services to confirm the position. She was informed that she was correct in requesting a medical certificate. Subsequently a rather unspecific letter from a private doctor was produced, which I attach (exhibit JE3).

I was naturally sorry that the children's relationship with the school terminated in such circumstances.

I make this statement conscientiously believing the same to be true and knowing that the same may be used in Court proceedings.